A Note to Parents and Caregivers:

Read-it! Joke Books are for children who are moving ahead on the amazing road to reading. These fun books support the acquisition and extension of reading skills as well as a love of books.

Published by the same company that produces *Read-it!* Readers, these books introduce the question/answer pattern that helps children expand their thinking about language structure and book formats.

When sharing a book with your child, read in short stretches, pausing often to talk about the pictures and the meaning of the book. The question/answer format works well for this purpose and provides an opportunity to talk about the language and meaning of the jokes. Have your child turn the pages and point to the pictures and familiar words. Read the story in a natural voice; have fun creating the voices of characters or emphasizing some important words. And be sure to reread favorite parts.

There is no right or wrong way to share books with children. Find time to read with your child, and pass on the legacy of literacy.

Adria F. Klein, Ph.D.
Professor Emeritus
California State University
San Bernardino, California

Managing Editor: Bob Temple

Creative Director: Terri Foley

Editors: Brenda Haugen, Nadia Higgins

Designer: John Moldstad

Page production: Picture Window Books

The illustrations in this book were prepared digitally.

Picture Window Books

5115 Excelsior Boulevard

Suite 232

Minneapolis, MN 55416

1-877-845-8392

www.picturewindowbooks.com

Printed in the United States of America.

Library of Congress Cataloging-in-Publication Data

Dahl, Michael.

Bell buzzers : a book of knock-knock jokes / written by Michael Dahl ; illustrated by Ryan Haugen.

p. cm. — (Read-it! joke books)

ISBN 1-4048-0236-3

1. Knock-knock jokes. I. Haugen, Ryan, 1972- ill. II. Title.

PN6231.K55D34 2003

818'.5402—dc21

2003004331

Bell Buzzers

A Book of Knock-Knock Jokes

Michael Dahl • Illustrated by Ryan Haugen

Reading Advisers:
Adria F. Klein, Ph.D.
Professor Emeritus, California State University
San Bernardino, California

Susan Kesselring, M.A., Literacy Educator
Rosemount-Apple Valley-Eagan (Minnesota) School District

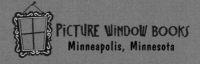

PICTURE WINDOW BOOKS
Minneapolis, Minnesota

Knock knock.
    Who's there?
Ben.
    Ben who?

Ben ringing this
bell all morning.

Knock knock.
  Who's there?
Apollo.
  Apollo who?

Apollo-gize for not
letting me in sooner!

Knock knock.
    Who's there?
Eddie.
    Eddie who?

Eddie body home?

Knock knock.
    Who's there?
Phillip.
    Phillip who?

Phillip my bag with candy!
Trick or treat!

8

Knock knock.
    Who's there?
Gladys.
    Gladys who?

Gladys you and not another monster.   9

Knock knock.
Who's there?
Doughnut.
Doughnut who?

Doughnut open the door!
There are monsters all around!   11

Knock knock.
Who's there?
Norma Lee.
Norma Lee who?

Norma Lee I don't buzz doorbells,
but I'm lost!

Knock knock.
Who's there?
Drew.
Drew who?

Drew you a picture.   13

Knock knock.
    Who's there?
Rhino.
    Rhino who?

Happy Birthday!

Rhino something you don't know.   **17**

Knock knock.
Who's there?
Ketchup.
Ketchup who?

Ketchup, or you'll
be left behind!

Knock knock.
   Who's there?
Cash.
   Cash who?

Cashew? I always thought
   you were a nut.

Knock knock.
    Who's there?
Howie.
    Howie who?

I'm fine, thanks. How are you?

Knock knock.
Who's there?
Peggy.
Peggy who?

Peggy me up after school, okay?

Knock knock.
   Who's there?
Patty O.
   Patty O. who?

Patty O'Furniture.

Knock knock.
Who's there?
Les.
Les who?

Les be friends.